NO ONE FIGHTS ALONE

PALMETTO
P U B L I S H I N G
Charleston, SC
www.PalmettoPublishing.com

TXu 2-388-228
Paperback ISBN: 979-8-8229-3052-0
eBook ISBN: 979-8-8229-3053-7

NO ONE FIGHTS ALONE

BRAD NEYENS

All my books are dedicated to my son Matthew. He passed away from suicide in 2021. I want to help bring awareness to this issue and do whatever I can to help. If you're ever considering suicide, please reach out for help. There's always another option. Matthew was one of the most creative minds I've ever encountered, so I'm writing these books to bring out my creative side to honor him.

A special thanks goes out to Kelly's Auto Body of Cedar Rapids, Iowa. They helped me fix my 370Z after a severe accident that totaled the car. One of my best memories was taking my son for rides in my 370Z. Thank you for helping me get my car back on the road. This way I can keep those memories alive with me.

Special thanks also goes out to Cassill Motors of Cedar Rapids, Iowa, for their help in continuing to build my 370Z, making it a car my son and I will be proud of.

Chapter One

———— · · · ————

It's late at night, and Brad and PJ are walking out of the gas station toward Mr. Daisuke and Brad's race car trailer, carrying food and beer. The gas station is very busy.

Across the parking lot in a semitrailer are Gabriel, Tom, Benito, and Jorge. Benito and Jorge are Gabriel's top two lieutenants. They are watching video monitors inside the back of Gabriel's custom semitrailer.

Tom asks Gabriel, "So what are you going to do with the man that killed your son?"

"We can take him out right here, boss," says Benito.

Gabriel tells Benito, "No, not quite yet. First, I want to kill everybody that he cares about. Then I'm going to crush him like the cockroach he is."

· · ·

Brad and PJ enter the back of their trailer and start to put the food away in a refrigerator.

Brad tells PJ, "I appreciate you letting me set up shop at your place until my new building is done."

PJ replies, "No problem, man. It's definitely going to be nice having some of your pizza again. Do you think you're going to be able to handle running Phil's Pizza and racing for Mr. Daisuke?"

"Yeah, I think I'll be fine. Rachel's been a big help," says Brad. "She's already found some contractors to start construction on the new building."

PJ finishes putting the beer in the fridge and then opens one up and starts to take a drink. Brad puts the rest of the groceries on the floor and then pulls a gun out from behind his back. He sticks it in PJ's back.

Brad tells him, "Give me your wallet."

PJ sets his beer on the countertop next to the fridge. PJ quickly takes action. PJ turns and grabs at the gun as a scuffle ensues. PJ ends up taking the gun away from Brad. He knocks Brad to the ground and shoots him twice in the chest with the gun he took from him. The gun is shooting paint markers. PJ offers his hand to help pick Brad up off the ground. Rex, PJ's dog, comes out of the sleeping area and sits down on the couch.

Brad asks PJ, "What did I do wrong this time?"

"You got a little too close."

Brad walks over to a dry-erase board by the refrigerator. It has their names on it. Brad erases the *15* next to PJ's name and writes *16*. There is a *10* next to Brad's name. Brad's phone starts to ring. It's his wife, Rachel.

Brad answers, "Hi, baby."

Rachel asks him, "So how much longer do you think you'll be?"

"Probably a few more days, but you already knew that, so what did you really call about?"

Rachel laughs. "Well, now that you are asking, I think I have changed my mind on the color scheme again. This will be the last time, I promise."

"I really don't care about the color scheme, babe," says Brad, sighing. "I'm just happy you agreed to help me."

"I found a new contractor that can start right away, and they're going to come in way under budget."

"That's great, babe. I can't wait to see how everything comes together. I better let you go, though. I really should get some rest before the race tomorrow."

"OK, I love you. Drive safe."

"I love you more."

Brad hangs up and looks over at PJ.

PJ tells him, "Thanks for letting Rex and me catch a ride with you. Josh and I should be done doing surveillance for Dennis this week."

"Well, do you think Josh has anything yet?" asks Brad.

PJ explains, "Dennis is a great guy, but his choice in women—he could definitely use a little bit of help. He seems to always find the women that love him for his money. I'm sure one of these days he's going to find the right one, and we'll be there to verify it for him."

"I'm so glad I won't have to worry about that."

Chapter Two

—— • • • ——

It's late at night, and Josh is in a surveillance van outside of a mansion. Josh is operating a small drone. The drone is looking through a second-floor window of the mansion. In the window is a young woman named Jade. Jade is a woman that Josh has been following for a couple days now. Jade is speaking to an older man. He hands her an envelope. After she takes it, she opens the envelope. She fans through the money. She places it on a small table next to her purse. Jade pushes the man back onto the bed. She slowly and seductively starts to remove her clothes as she comes closer to the bed. Back in the van, Josh is typing on a laptop, giving the description, the time, and place. Josh starts pulling still pictures off the video and puts them into a file.

Josh texts PJ and tells him, "I definitely think I have everything we need for Dennis. I am wrapping things up here now."

· · ·

The next morning, back at the empty lot where Phil's Pizza used to be, there is a semitruck dropping off building materials. Rachel is standing next to a drafting table, looking at the blueprints. Rachel's phone starts to ring; it's Brad, calling from the track before the races start.

Rachel answers, "Hey, baby."

"Hey, sexy, we're getting ready to start and will be done shortly. Josh and PJ are finishing up doing their thing. We should be home late afternoon tomorrow."

"Can't wait to see you, baby. Why don't you grab the rest of the food on the way into town? I don't think I'm going to have time to pick it up. I have the plumber coming by tomorrow."

Mr. Daisuke, Brad's race team owner, waves Brad over. They are ready for him at the starting line.

Brad acknowledges that he sees Mr. Daisuke and starts walking over. "Sounds like a plan, baby. I got to go; they're ready for me."

Brad hangs up the phone as he walks over to the race car. Mr. Daisuke hands Brad his helmet as he's getting in the car.

Mr. Daisuke tells him, "We're going to give them a minute head start this time. Think you can handle that?"

Brad laughs. "Only a minute this time? You're slipping."

"Well, you do only have two laps to catch him on this race," Mr. Daisuke tells him. "Keep an eye out. He tried cheating against your dad many years ago. I think he might try something."

"This one is definitely going to be interesting. So, how's your progress coming on the electric conversion?"

Mr. Daisuke pats him on the back. "Why don't you let me worry about the cars? You just worry about the four mil we have on the line for this race."

Brad starts the GTR as Mr. Daisuke steps back and pulls a stopwatch from his pocket. Brad pulls over to the starting line. The race starts as the green light goes off. A high-end exotic accelerates from the starting line as Brad remains in place. Mr. Daisuke points at Brad after a minute goes by.

Brad takes off to catch the high-end exotic. He accelerates and tears up the track quickly. He is closing in on the high-end exotic. As he comes within reach, they complete the first lap. He is only about two cars back. Brad is getting closer halfway through the second lap. The front bumper of the GTR is almost right at the rear bumper of the high-end exotic.

The driver sees that Brad's getting ready to pass and presses a small button under his dash that shoots out steel ball bearings from below his back bumper. The ball bearings bounce off the track, slamming into Brad's car, and one hits his intercooler. A couple of the bearings hit Brad's windshield, cracking it severely. Brad manages to cross the finish line, beating the exotic by about one car length but with notable damage to the GTR. Brad makes his way back into the pits and parks the car. The pit crew starts assessing the damage done to the car. They show Lee, the head of Mr. Daisuke's pit crew, parts that have been damaged. One of the pit crew members removes one of the ball bearings from the front-mount intercooler. He gives it to Lee. Lee approaches Mr. Daisuke and hands him the ball bearing.

"I have a rough list of what needs replaced," Lee tells him. He starts to read from a small piece of paper. "Repair or replace the front-mount intercooler. Repair or replace the front bumper; replace the windshield. We should just give it a once-over at the shop. There's too much that could be wrong, Mr. Daisuke."

Brad is irritated as he gets out of the car and walks over to Mr. Daisuke. "Well, you were right. Now if you will excuse me, I have to go have a little chat with Ricky's driver."

Brad passes by Ricky as Ricky walks over to Mr. Daisuke. He hands him a check and shakes his hand.

Ricky says, "Man, you have got yourself one hell of a driver there. Shane promised me he was going to win."

Mr. Daisuke shakes his head. "I really hope this is none of your doing, Ricky." He hands a small ball bearing over to Ricky and continues. "I'll get you a list of repairs needed for my car shortly. My new partner is going to have a little chat with your driver."

"Shane did this?" asks Ricky.

Mr. Daisuke tells him, "He pulled some shady shit in the past against Phil years ago. I'd have to go back to the video to confirm, but I think you just hired the driver that would do anything to win for you. As for Brad, he definitely knows."

Brad walks up to Shane as he's getting out of the high-end exotic car. "Did you think that shit was funny?" he says.

"Why do you care? You still won."

Brad gets up in Shane's face. Shane pushes him back and takes a swing at him. Brad counters. He has clearly been training with PJ for a while and deals with him very easily. The punch Shane has thrown is used quickly against him. Brad uses his momentum against Shane and puts him down using his own arm, then shoves him to the ground using his arm for leverage.

Brad tells him, "You keep fucking around and you'll find out what happens next."

He applies more pressure to Shane's arm, causing him to scream out in pain.

Shane relents. "OK. OK."

Brad lets Shane's arm go and helps him up. One of Shane's crew members, Michael, walks up to another and taps him on the shoulder. He asks the crew member in sign language, "What's going on?"

Another crew member, Jeff, signs back, "Brad didn't take too kindly to Shane trying to cheat."

"I told that asshole he shouldn't do that."

"Well, now Brad told Shane if he keeps fucking around, he'll find out."

Brad signs back, "See you next time, guys."

"I like him. He's good people," Michael says.

Brad starts walking back to his race team. Shane tries to play it off like he's fine as the rest of his crew starts to laugh at him. Brad's phone starts to ring. He picks it up.

PJ is on the line. "Hey, we're almost done here. We should be at the track in about twenty minutes."

Brad tells him, "Great, we can hit the road as soon as we load everything up here. We can move that Monday meeting to your place while we have the barbecue."

"You know there's a meeting next Wednesday. I can always go to that one."

"Yeah, and we can go to that one too."

PJ chuckles a little bit and replies, "You know, you don't have to go to every meeting with me. I can handle it."

"I know, but I like being there," Brad explains. "And it gives me a little more time to get some more training in. I even got to use some of the new Krav Maga that you have been showing me. I can't wait to tell the guys about it. I'm looking forward to learning the next new fighting style."

PJ says, "I'm looking forward to teaching you Jiu Jitsu."

Brad and PJ both hang up their phones.

Chapter Three

———— · · · ————

PJ and Josh are sitting in Dennis's waiting room by the secretary. Josh is carrying a small folder full of information, including photos with a USB drive.

Dennis's secretary, Mabel, looks over at PJ. "Dennis is ready for you now."

A small group of people are leaving Dennis's office. PJ and Josh stand up and head into his office. Dennis greets them and shakes their hands.

Dennis asks, "So what did you guys find out?"

Josh starts his presentation to Dennis. "After two days of surveilling Jade, on day two I observed her entering a residential home. As you can see from the photos and the time stamps, she was not going to see her family as she said she was going to. Which confirms your suspicions. I have the full video on the USB drive from our drone, but as the still pictures I pulled from the video show, you can see clearly that she is not being faithful."

Dennis responds, "I hate being right."

He picks up his phone and calls Mabel. "Could you please issue a check for Tier One Security? Then can you please have Mark come to my office? I'm not going to need this ring anymore."

Dennis hangs up the phone and stands up and shakes PJ's and Josh's hands.

"Thank you, gentlemen, for doing such a thorough job."

Dennis sits back down. He opens one of his desk drawers, pulls out a small ring box, and sets it on his desk.

PJ and Josh walk out of Dennis's office and over to Mabel's desk.

• • •

Brad is talking to Mr. Daisuke while the race team is finishing loading up the race car. PJ and Josh pull up in their surveillance van.

Mr. Daisuke tells Brad, "If you want to head out early, we can finish up here and meet you back at the hotel."

Brad says, "All right, let me know how the repairs go."

Brad walks over to PJ and Josh as they pull in.

Brad says, "So what do you guys think of the new surveillance van?"

"You know you didn't have to buy it for us," says PJ.

"I have to pull my weight in this partnership somehow," Brad answers. He gets in the vehicle. "Let's head back to the hotel, and we can leave early tomorrow morning. Rachel wants me to pick up the food for the barbecue on the way back into town."

Chapter Four

Rachel is at a table inside PJ's gun range, looking over the blueprints for the pizza shop. Tiffany, PJ's business partner, comes over.

"Are you guys excited to design your own building?" Tiffany asks. "I know Travis was. He liked having the ability to build in extra security."

Rachel looks over at her. "Do you really think I should do that?"

"It's a very dangerous world we live in, and you need to be prepared for anything."

Tiffany walks around the display case and presses a button, which quickly transforms the top of the display case into a bulletproof barrier.

Rachel is surprised. "Oh my God, that's so cool. Brad would love to have something like that."

Tiffany says, "PJ and I have a guy that specializes in custom work like this. I can see if he would like to do some work at your new place."

"That would be great, especially after everything that happened to Brad's parents. I can only think that if Phil and Peggy had had something like that, just maybe they would still be with us."

Tiffany presses another button on the display case, lowering it back into place. A few seconds after the display case is lowered, the door opens, and the doorbell goes off. Rachel's new contractor walks in. He is an athletic-looking Hispanic man in his midtwenties. He walks over to Rachel, where the blueprints are laid out.

He begins to talk. "From the looks of it, I must be in the right place." He extends his hand to shake and continues. "You must be Rachel; we spoke on the phone. I'm Benito."

After shaking Rachel's hand, he receives a text alert.

"Oh, the joys of running your own business. Do you mind if I respond to this real quick?"

"Not at all, please take a moment."

Benito looks at his phone. The message is from Gabriel.

"Let me know how the meeting goes," it says. "I will let you know when we can move forward on taking the girl."

Benito responds to the text, saying, "Will do, boss."

Chapter Five

— • • • —

Back at Mr. Daisuke's race shop, Brad's race car is being unloaded from the back of a semitrailer. Lee starts the GTR and drives it out of the back of the semitrailer. The windshield has a big crack in it. Mr. Daisuke walks up as Lee parks the car in one of the maintenance bays.

Mr. Daisuke tells him, "Once you get an updated list of repairs needed, could you please bring it to my office? The windshield really concerns me. We need to make sure this doesn't happen again."

"What were you thinking? Maybe something shatter resistant? It's probably going to add some extra weight."

"We can handle the extra weight. I can't, however, have Brad getting hurt. Why don't we just go ahead and add a roll cage? Lose the interior and just convert it to a full race car. Brad isn't driving the GTR every day like his dad would have."

Mr. Daisuke receives a text alert. He pulls the phone from his pocket and looks at it. It is Brad.

"I know you guys are probably busy working on the car," Brad has texted him, "but I wanted to remind you of the barbecue tonight. It will start around six if you and the guys want to come by Tier One Tactical. Good friends and cold beer. Hope to see you guys there."

He texts Brad back, "We'll be there, looking forward to it."

Chapter Six

— — — · · · — — —

Brad, PJ, and Josh are at the local Hy-Vee grocery store. Brad and PJ are waiting in line with a cart that is overflowing with supplies for the barbecue Brad is putting together. PJ notices four shady-looking men walk in the front of the store and instantly spread out. One of the men is sharply dressed and talking on his phone. He seems to be directing the other three men. Two men with athletic builds, wearing jeans and T-shirts, get in line behind Brad and PJ. One is noticeably taller than the other, and they have no groceries. They appear out of place and very suspicious. None of the other shoppers seem to notice that the men are in line with no groceries.

PJ leans over to Brad and whispers in his ear, "I think there's something about to go down. Be ready for anything. Four possible assailants. One and two are the two men behind us; the third one is the heavier-set Hispanic man over by the magazines. The fourth one is on his cell phone at the corner, by the flowers."

Brad whispers back, "So, we should take care of the guys behind us first?"

PJ nods his head.

A few seconds go by. Then Jorge nods his head to the man by the magazines, who then proceeds to pull a gun and yell out, "This is a robbery." He shoots his gun into the air. He grabs the nearest cashier.

As the two men behind Brad and PJ draw their weapons, PJ, and Brad spring into action. They quickly take down the two men behind them and use their own guns to shoot them. They turn and simultaneously shoot at the third man holding the gun at the cashier. They deal with him very easily, before he can react. PJ turns his attention to Jorge, who is quickly fleeing the scene, getting into a Ford Mustang and speeding away. Josh comes around the corner of one of the grocery aisles, carrying more groceries. He sees what's going on and draws his handgun to help back up Brad.

PJ looks over at Brad and Josh. "You got them?"

Brad says, "Yeah."

PJ heads out the front door in pursuit and watches the Mustang speed out of the parking lot. Brad pulls his cell phone from his pocket while his assailants are bleeding on the ground.

Josh asks one of the men that is still conscious, "Do you have any other weapons on you?"

"Fuck you," the man replies with blood coming from his mouth. He starts to pass out and then succumbs to his injuries.

Brad speed-dials Captain Charlie, who picks up his phone while he is sitting in his office at the station.

Brad says, "Hey, Charlie, you're probably going to need to make your way down here to Hy-Vee. PJ and I just stopped a robbery attempt. I can explain when you get here."

At that moment another officer comes to Captain Charlie's office. "Charlie, there's been a shooting at Hy-Vee, and there's three presumed dead on the scene."

Charlie responds to Brad, "I guess I'll be seeing you guys in a little bit, then."

Brad asks him, "Think we can wrap this up pretty quick? I have to start cooking for tonight."

Captain Charlie responds very sarcastically, "Yeah, I'll see what I can do."

Brad looks over at Josh and says, "Remind me to take some food to Charlie after I am done cooking."

Brad starts to find Rachel's name on his speed dial. He presses send and texts her.

Brad, using his speech-to-text function, tells her, "Hey, baby, I think we're going to be a little bit later than I thought."

Chapter Seven

· · ·

Outside of town Gabriel's tractor-trailer is parked on the side of an old country road. The Ford Mustang that left the robbery attempt at Hy-Vee pulls up behind the semitrailer, and Jorge gets out of the car. Two men get out of the back of the semitrailer with gas cans and start to pour gas inside and outside of the car while Jorge gets into the back of the semitrailer. One of the men lights the car on fire. The two men get back into the semitrailer and start to drive away, leaving the car engulfed in flames.

Jorge is sitting at a table with Gabriel, eating seafood. "Boss, you were right. These guys will not be easy."

Gabriel tears open a lobster tail. He starts to dip it in butter. "Looks like we're going to have to go with your brother's plan, then."

Gabriel starts to eat more of his food. He looks at the men. "Sit down, guys; eat. We have a long night ahead of us. Jorge, call your brother and tell him we're going to be moving forward with his plan shortly."

Jorge asks him, "Boss, why don't we just shoot them from a distance and be done with this?"

"He made it personal the way he killed my son," says Gabriel, "and I want to look him in the face as I take his life."

Jorge nods his head. "I understand, boss. Let my brother and me finish this for you." He pulls out his phone and calls his brother.

Benito answers the phone. "Please tell me that it's done and we can go home now," he says.

"I wish I could, bro, but they have clearly been trained. They took out three of my best soldiers very easily. It looks like you might have an opportunity to put your plan in motion."

Gabriel is pulling out a folder with pictures of Brad and Rachel in it. He yells out to Jorge, "Make sure he doesn't hurt the redhead. I want to put her to work."

Jorge tells Benito, "Try not to hurt the redhead. The boss wants to put her to work."

Benito says, "I can see that. Hell, I might have to break her in before we take her back to Mexico."

"Let's worry about the task at hand first," Jorge laughs. "You didn't see how fast they took out my men. These guys will not go down easily."

Chapter Eight

— • • • —

Brad is tending to the grill at the Tier One Tactical Gun Range. He is making food for everybody.

Tiffany is talking to PJ. "Seriously, you can't even go grocery shopping without killing someone."

PJ laughs at Tiffany. "It wasn't all me. He helped too."

PJ gets up and walks over to Brad and smacks Brad in the back of the head lightly. "Is it about time to eat?"

Josh calls out, "Please don't overcook mine."

"Why don't you guys stop picking on my man?" says Rachel. She walks over to Brad and gives him a big hug and kiss. Tiffany comes out from the back door of the building. She walks over to Rachel and Brad.

Tiffany tells Rachel, "Dalton agreed to come by and look at your guys' project. He'll be here in just a little bit."

Brad starts putting food on plates. "All right, come and get it, everybody."

Lee walks up and grabs one of the plates that Brad is handing out. "We're going to be making some big changes to the car," he says. "We're going to lose the interior and put in a roll cage."

"Can you do something with the windshield?" says Brad. "That's really the only thing that concerns me."

Mr. Daisuke picks up a plate and joins the conversation. "Yes, we're looking into some pretty cool stuff for the windshield, and the doors as well."

As Tiffany walks up to grab her plate of food, her phone goes off with a text message. She pulls it out of her back pocket and starts to read it. It's from one of her friends at the CIA.

The text reads, "We lost track of Gabriel and his two new top lieutenants crossing the border earlier Monday morning. There also has been a lot of chatter about Gabriel wanting to get revenge for the loss of his son. His main target seems to be PJ and anybody that he's close to. NO MATTER THE COST."

Tiffany calls over to PJ to look at the text. "PJ, you don't think what happened earlier at Hy-Vee was Gabriel, do you?"

PJ replies, "Well, I didn't until now. I think we got really lucky. I thought I was done with this shit, but now it's at my front door. I need to bring everybody up to speed, to let them know they're in danger. I don't want to see any more of my friends getting hurt." PJ raises his voice and yells out, "Everybody gather around. I need to tell you guys something."

Tiffany shuts off the music playing in the background. Everybody gathers in a circle around the firepit and starts listening to PJ.

He starts, "What happened today was extremely serious, and I just now found out how serious it might have really been. There is a war coming. This isn't your fight. It's my fight. I know what's coming all too well; he is relentless and will not stop until he gets what he wants. He has more resources at his disposal. If he wants a fight, he's going to bring that fight to me. So, everybody needs to clear out. I don't want any of you getting hurt."

Brad walks over to PJ. "I'm not going to let you do this on your own. I may not have spent the last twenty years fighting alongside you, but I'm here now, and I got your six."

Mr. Daisuke stands up from his chair and walks over to PJ and Brad. "Are these the same men that took Phil and Peggy away from us?" he asks.

PJ says, "They all take orders from the same cartel."

"Well, I might not be able to handle myself in a gunfight," says Mr. Daisuke, "but I do know war can cost a fortune. And if a fortune is what it's going to take to win this war, you and Brad have a blank check. Whatever you guys need; I can get it for you."

All the men from PJ's therapy group stand up and walk over to Brad, PJ, and Mr. Daisuke.

Tyler says, "Are you guys seriously thinking about doing this without us? I'm here to tell you that shit is not a fucking option. Nobody fights alone."

Tyler holds out his hand, and everybody from the therapy group starts putting their cell phones in Tyler's hands. Tyler drops all of them into the fire. Then PJ, Brad, and Mr. Daisuke proceed to throw their phones into the fire as well.

Josh starts laughing at everybody. "You guys know I could have just gone through everybody's phones and made sure nobody was tracking us, right?" Then Josh throws his phone into the fire as well. "I just want y'all to know that was a brand-new phone. No cracked screen—hell, I haven't even dropped it yet."

The cell phones start to explode in the fire. Josh looks over at Brad. "Lithium batteries. I can't believe you actually want to drive a race car with one of those things in it."

Tiffany walks to the firepit and throws her phone in as well. Dalton pulls into the parking lot and walks over to join the barbecue. Tiffany walks over to greet him.

Chapter Nine

- - -

Inside Gabriel's custom semitrailer, Gabriel is talking to Jorge.

"Jorge, at 9:45, right after they open, make sure PJ and that bitch from the CIA are in the building. Use the M249 SAW, and then burn that building to the ground when you're done. Make sure nobody leaves that building alive. Benito, grab the girl after your brother starts at PJ's place. I'm going to call in Luis and his crew to take out the kid while he's driving."

Benito responds, "Will do, boss. We'll see you at the plane soon."

Jorge speaks up. "It's going to be my pleasure killing these two for you, boss."

- - -

Back at Mr. Daisuke's shop are Lee and Dalton; they are finishing up some last-minute modifications to Brad's race car. Lee is wiping down the windshield. Josh sticks his head out of the back door of the semitrailer as Lee and Dalton begin to load Brad's race car. Josh, with a virtual reality headset on, is steering an RC car around the shop.

Josh yells out to Brad, "I got all the new gear installed. When do you want to try out the new controls?"

Brad is looking at pictures of the racetrack. He is studying the corners and where to break. "After we get to the track."

Jim, one of Brad's and PJ's friends from the therapy group, is sitting next to him. He's cleaning his gun. Jim stops cleaning his gun as he sees Brad starting to put away all his pictures of the racetrack. "PJ wanted you to have this," he says.

He bends down and opens a duffel bag by his feet and pulls out a handgun case. He puts it on the table in front of Brad. Brad opens the gun case up. Inside there is a highly customized .40-caliber handgun.

There is a note from PJ: "I hope you enjoy the modifications I've done. Be ready for anything."

Brad clears his new gun. He puts the fully loaded magazine in the gun and chambers a round. Then he puts the new gun in the custom holster that's in the box.

Brad stands up, pulls off his old gun and holster, and replaces it with the new one. There's a small ankle holster for his original gun, and he puts that on and puts the other gun in it. Jim pulls two ballistic vests out of the duffel bag, slides one over to Brad, and puts on the other one.

Brad tells him, "That's OK, I have my gear in the car. Give that one to Josh."

Mr. Daisuke comes out of his office and walks over to Brad and Jim. "OK, I worked out all the details for the race. Let me tell you, this is going to be a big one. We're going to do a two-lap race, and you must beat them by thirty seconds. Now I know you like to chase them down for the win, but these guys are going to try to get in your head. And I figured, why not have some fun with it? You could blow off some steam, and since we added the roll cage and stiffened up the chassis, it's going to give us the ability to put the hottest tune I've ever had the opportunity to run in one of my cars. I can't wait to see you on the track with this new setup."

Chapter Ten

─────── • • • ───────

Brad's on the phone, talking to Rachel, as his team unloads his car from the trailer. "How is everything going, baby?"

Rachel tells him, "Everything's good here, babe. I know that you want me to stay at home with the extra security you got for me, but the contractor called, and he needs me down at the construction site to meet with the inspector around 10:00. He said he had a few questions, and it shouldn't take but a few minutes. Is it OK to go down there and see them?"

Brad says, "I don't know, baby; I really don't want anything to happen to you. Greg and Danny both agree that there's too many variables if you are out in public."

"It will be fine, baby," says Rachel. "He said it should take only about fifteen minutes."

Brad relents. "OK, let me talk to Greg and Danny."

Rachel puts the phone on speaker. "OK, I got you on speaker, baby."

"Are you guys OK with taking her down there?" Brad asks.

Greg tells Brad, "We checked out the contractor earlier, and they are relatively new in the area and haven't done very many jobs. That concerns us a little bit, but we can limit our time on site to try to minimize her exposure in the open."

Brad starts to talk to Rachel. "OK, baby, I trust Greg and Danny to keep you safe. Make sure you listen to them. Remember everything PJ told you. Make sure to wear that belt that he gave you. Do you remember what to do if they use the code phrase?"

Rachel says, "Yes, and we'll be fine."

Lee waves over Brad so he can test the car before the race. Brad tells her, "I got to go; they're ready for me, baby. Greg, Danny, thanks again for doing this on such short notice."

Rachel says, "I love you, baby, and good luck at the race today."

Brad hangs up the phone and starts to walk over to his car. Josh pulls up next to Brad in his surveillance van. "I'll have the new drone overhead in about ten minutes," he says, "to provide overwatch."

• • •

Back at Tier One Tactical Gun Range, Tiffany is sitting at a desk, watching a live video from above their gun range. She's geared up for war with tactical wear.

"How are things looking out there, Tyler?"

Tyler is in the field about two hundred yards away from the building. He is wearing a ghillie suit and blends in very well to his surroundings. He's on the ground surveying the area with his rifle in his hand.

Tyler tells her, "Everything looks quiet out here. Little to no traffic. But that van concerns me. It pulled up about a thousand meters to the east down the road at 0100, and it's been sitting there idling the whole time. I can see two people in it."

Tiffany rotates the drone overhead to find the van. The camera comes to a stop as a sports car pulls up behind the van. Both vehicles start moving down the street toward Tier One Tactical Gun Range.

Tiffany declares, "Looks like it might be showtime."

PJ comes around the corner with Rex at his feet. "Well, if I was going to try to kill me, I would probably do it before I finished my morning coffee too."

He looks down at his watch as the timer starts to go off. He shuts it off and walks over to the front windows. He turns on the "open" sign.

Tiffany tells him, "Looks like we're about to have company. They're starting to pull up out front."

"Ready to engage," says Tyler.

PJ says, "Let's see what these new toys can do first."

Tiffany reaches for a small case from under the counter, and then she walks out the back door. She opens the case and sets it on the ground. There are four small drones in the case. The drones are about the size of a small cell phone. She presses a small button in the middle of all the drones, and they all start up and take off from the case. She shuts the case and takes it back inside.

PJ tells her, "I really hope your new toys are worth the money that Mr. Daisuke paid for them."

"This kind of tech is going to change the world forever," says Tiffany. She opens her laptop and opens a file on it. Four camera feeds from the drones pop up on her laptop screen. The top of the screen reads "Facial recognition active." The drones are gaining elevation and then stop hovering around one hundred meters above the building. The camera feed finds three individuals in front of the building and starts scanning their faces. Their faces slowly start to pop up on the bottom of the screen as they exit their vehicles. The facial recognition software is finding them in the database. One of the individuals is wanted for murder in multiple cities.

Outside, Jorge parks behind the van and gets out. He starts to have a conversation with the driver of the van, a Hispanic man in his midtwenties. The van driver gets out and walks toward the building. Once inside, he starts to walk around the store, looking at items. He pulls out his phone and looks at two pictures—one is PJ, the other Tiffany—to confirm their identity.

PJ says, "Is there anything I can help you with?"

The man tells him, "I'm good; I was just checking on some prices. Maybe next payday I can afford it," as he points to one of the guns in the display case.

He smiles at PJ, turns, and walks out the door. As the door shuts behind him, PJ presses a small button on the display case. He has modified his display case into a bulletproof barrier. He takes a drink of his coffee and looks over at Tiffany.

"I hope your new toys are ready, because he definitely knows it's us," he tells her.

Tiffany is staring at her laptop screen, watching the man who has exited the building. He gives Jorge a thumbs-up. Jorge opens the van door facing the building and pulls out a late machine gun. He starts to shoot the building. Bullets are tearing into the wall repeatedly as PJ sips on his coffee. Rex remains by PJ's side. A few bullets eventually make it through the reinforced bulletproof wall and hit the barrier in front of PJ and Tiffany.

Jorge continues to fire, and the other two men grab gas cans out of the van. The two men walk over to each side of the building as Jorge continues to shoot bullets into the building randomly. Tiffany starts typing on her laptop. Three of the four drones stop hovering and target the three men. They start flying directly toward their heads, then crash into all three of the men's heads and explode on impact, killing them instantly.

PJ asks Tyler, "How's it looking out there?"

Tyler says, "All three targets are down; no movement."

PJ picks up a phone to call Brad.

Chapter Eleven

· · ·

Brad's new cell phone is sitting inside the surveillance van next to Josh. Josh is using a virtual reality headset to control a drone. The drone is hovering above Brad's race car. As the race starts, a phone call pops up on his display.

Josh answers Brad's phone. "Hey, PJ how's it going? Brad's just getting ready to start."

The lights change on the starting line, letting Brad and the other driver start the race. Josh is trying his best to keep up with the cars, with the drone following behind. He starts increasing the drone's elevation to survey the track in front of Brad. Brad quickly gets a lead on his opponent.

PJ tells Josh, "They just came for us here. How are things looking on your guys' end?"

Josh says, "Everything looks good here. Is there anything special I should be looking for?"

"Just keep an eye out for anything out of place or people that are not supposed to be there," PJ instructs him.

"OK."

Brad is on a wireless earpiece and chimes in on the conversation. "Everybody OK?"

"Yeah," says PJ. "We're good here. I was going to go and support Greg and Danny as soon as the cops finish up here." Tiffany is next to PJ, calling the cops.

Brad says, "I appreciate that. She was going to be heading down to meet with the new contractor. They needed her there for the inspector for something."

"I'm going to head over now," says PJ.

Brad tells him, "Thank you. I don't know what I would do if I lost her too."

Brad has the finish line in his sights, with a substantial lead on his opponent. At that moment a .308 round strikes the windshield in front of him. The bullet doesn't penetrate the windshield.

Brad yells, "I'm under fire!"

PJ tells him, "I'm on my way."

"I will meet you at the Jeep," Tyler tells PJ.

PJ grabs a go bag and his rifle from behind the counter that he's standing in front of. He starts to head toward the front door. Rex starts to head out with PJ.

PJ turns and tells the dog, "Stay with Tiffany, Rex."

Brad says, "PJ, go to Rachel and make sure she's safe. We can handle this."

Brad starts taking evasive maneuvers as another round strikes the windshield.

Josh says, "I don't see anything yet."

Josh starts to maneuver the drone higher and higher, and he finally sees a man on top of a hill, leaning against a car with a long rifle.

Josh tells Brad, "North of your position, there's a car with a single shooter."

Brad crosses the finish line as a third round strikes the windshield. "Josh," he says, "get him to shoot at the drone. I need time to get out of the car."

Brad grabs a backpack from the passenger-side seat. Josh starts flying the drone directly at the shooter on the hill. As the drone comes closer to the shooter, the shooter takes his eyes off Brad and starts to shoot at the drone. Brad jumps out of the car, letting the car continue rolling ahead as he runs for cover. He puts the backpack on and pulls it up over his chest, converting it into a ballistic vest. It has a tactical AR-15 strapped to the front of it and AR-15 magazines.

Josh starts to maneuver the drone erratically as he gets closer to the shooter. The shooter continues to shoot at the drone. He manages to hit it, and the drone falls about twenty feet in front of the shooter's car. Then he directs his attention back toward Brad and his car. The shooter frantically looks through his scope but can't find Brad in the car. He suddenly sees a reflection off of Brad's scope.

Brad starts to line up his shot, taking a deep breath and then slowly exhaling. He squeezes off one round quickly, followed up by a second shot. The shooter takes one round to the right hand and the gun he is holding. The second round strikes him in the head, downing him instantly. Josh maneuvers the camera from the downed drone to see if the shooter is down.

Josh tells everyone, "Shooter looks to be down; no movement."

Chapter Twelve

- - -

Greg is driving an SUV with Danny sitting in the back seat next to Rachel. They pull in to the construction site. There are four construction workers building a wall for the new building. Multiple piles of wood waiting to be used surround the work site. Benito and another man are standing at the drafting table, looking over blueprints. Greg pulls in and parks the SUV. Greg and Danny both get out of the SUV, and then Rachel. Greg's phone starts to ring as he shuts the door on the SUV. Rachel and Danny start walking over to the two men standing at the drafting table. Greg looks at his phone. The caller ID says it's Tiffany.

As he answers the phone, Tiffany tells him, "They just tried to hit us here. Now they're trying to go after Brad. PJ and Tyler are en route to you guys now."

Rachel arrives at the drafting table and starts talking to the two men.

Greg hangs up his phone. He looks over at Danny and says, "So where do you want to go to eat lunch?"

Rachel turns and looks at Danny, concerned. Danny grabs her by the hand and starts to pull her back to the SUV. At that moment Benito grabs Rachel by the other arm. The other man at the drafting table pulls out a gun and starts to point it at Danny. The four men that were building the wall drop their tools and pick up some guns that were hidden behind a small woodpile. All four start to open fire on Greg.

Greg reaches out for Rachel at the front of the SUV. He takes a bullet to his left hand, then quickly retreats for cover behind the SUV. The men continue to shoot at him, and he opens an app on his phone and keys in a four-digit code. The driver- and passenger-side back windows of the SUV tilt out. Six small launchers appear. Tear gas and smoke grenades automatically start launching out of the back windows of the SUV.

Danny quickly deals with the man holding the gun on him, disarming him, and knocking him to the ground. Then he pulls out his own gun and shoots the man twice in the chest. He quickly pulls Rachel close to him as he puts his body in between Benito and Rachel. Benito draws a firearm from his waistband and shoots

Danny in the back twice as Danny pushes Rachel toward Greg and the SUV.

Danny yells at Rachel, "Get to Greg."

Rachel starts running toward the SUV. Danny turns and starts to return fire as Benito stabs him twice in the back with a tactical knife underneath his bulletproof vest. Danny tries to raise his gun to shoot Benito as he tries to turn around. Benito grabs his arm as Danny manages to squeeze off two rounds from his handgun. Benito has been hit in the left leg twice. Benito knocks the gun out of Danny's hand and begins to twist the knife. Danny cries out in excruciating pain. Then Benito punches him and knocks him unconscious.

The four men continue to rain down bullets toward the SUV as Greg opens the back door. Greg flips the seat, revealing a small cabinet full of guns and tactical equipment. He grabs an AR-15 and starts to return fire on the four men. Then he reaches into the cabinet and presses a button, releasing a small drone from the back window. The drone immediately climbs up one hundred meters and begins to hover. It automatically starts performing facial recognition and takes video and pictures, relaying all that information back to Greg's cell phone.

Greg downs one of the four men who are shooting at him when the man tries to flank him at the SUV. Greg throws a grenade over the SUV, close to the three remaining men. They scatter, giving him an opportunity to shoot and down another one.

Benito catches up to Rachel and tackles her to the ground. He picks Rachel up and puts his bloody knife to her throat. "Keep fighting me," he says to her, "and I'm going to take that pretty little head of yours clean off."

Two SUVs pull up from the street. Benito opens the door on the first SUV. He shoves Rachel into the back seat and gets in behind her. It drives away. The two remaining gunmen make a run for the second SUV. Greg sees an opportunity to take them out and starts shooting. He takes them both down very quickly. The driver returns fire, striking Greg in the shoulder. The SUV starts to drive away. Greg continues shooting through the windshield, causing the driver to swerve and drive into a woodpile. The driver gets out and starts shooting back at Greg.

Down the road PJ's Jeep appears, speeding toward the construction site. Tyler leans out the passenger-side window. Tyler aims his rifle down the road at the driver shooting at Greg. He takes one squeeze of the trigger, and he downs the driver with a single shot. PJ starts to call for help.

The dispatcher says, "Nine-one-one, what's your emergency?"

"I need an ambulance sent to Phil's Pizza."

He parks the Jeep right next to Greg and Danny's SUV. Tyler and PJ both jump out of the Jeep and start to administer first aid to Greg and Danny, trying to stop the bleeding.

Greg hands PJ his cell phone. "Our drone should have recorded everything. I'm sure I don't need to remind you what's going to happen to her if they get her out of the country."

.   .   .

Benito calls Gabriel after fleeing the scene from an old country road. "Boss, I have the girl, but I don't think the rest of my guys made it out of there. She had some private security with her. I did not anticipate that level of security. Have you heard from Jorge? He's not responding to my text."

Gabriel tells him, "No, but your brother knew the risks of going after PJ directly. I haven't heard anything from the team I sent to take out the kid either. You always thought three moves ahead, and that's why my empire can be yours now if you bring me my son's killer. You've seen the value of having leverage, and that's why you wanted to go after the girl. I have another crew coming into town. I instructed them to follow your lead. They're going to be at the downtown farmers' market tomorrow. Now bring me my son's killer. I only care about the man

49

that took my son from me. Everybody else will just be collateral damage."

"I'll bring him to you so you can have the pleasure of killing him yourself," says Benito. "I will use the girl to get him for you." He hangs up the phone and puts the knife closer to Rachel's throat, cutting her slightly. "I need you to have your man bring PJ to me."

Benito holds out his hand, and the driver of the SUV hands him a piece of paper for Rachel to read from. He hands it to Rachel. "Read this."

Benito starts recording a video. Rachel starts to read what's on the paper to herself and starts to break down and cry. She looks at him. "How can I read this to my husband?"

"You're only good to me if your man can bring me PJ. Otherwise, you better believe everything in that letter is going to happen if PJ doesn't show up."

He starts recording with his phone. Rachel starts to read from the letter. "These are the last words you'll ever hear from me unless you have PJ come with us unarmed. They are willing to trade me for PJ at the farmers' market at 11:45 tomorrow. Or I will be put to work. They will call you tomorrow at 11:45 sharp with further instructions. Ask PJ what I mean by put to work."

Benito reaches over with his knife and cuts open Rachel's top, exposing her bra. Rachel tries to stop him from cutting more of her top; then he cuts her on the arm. Benito stops the video. The driver of the SUV throws Rachel a new tank top, and she puts it on quickly.

Chapter Thirteen

⸻ • • • ⸻

Brad stands up from the concrete barrier that he was taking cover behind at the racetrack after shooting the gunman. He starts walking back to the car, which came to a stop next to the guardrail off the track. As he approaches his car, Josh's voice comes over his headset. "I think the gunman's cell phone is starting to ring."

A few seconds go by. On one of the many surveillance cameras attached to the van, Josh notices an SUV coming around a small building in the pits. "I don't think we're done yet, boys," he says. "We have four more shooters getting out of the SUV that just pulled up."

The men pile out of the SUV, armed with assault rifles and body armor. They start shooting at the surveillance van. Everybody in the pit area starts scrambling for cover to get out of the line of fire.

Jim immediately stands up and yells at Josh, "Do not leave this van." Jim climbs out the side door and quickly finds cover behind the front of a race car about fifteen feet away from the surveillance van. He starts to return fire and downs one of the four men with his first shot. Josh grabs a small briefcase from a cabinet inside the surveillance van and opens it. Inside there are four small drones. Josh presses a small button in the center of the drones, and they start to hover inside the van. Josh opens the back door of the van, and they start to fly out the back door and climb through the air until they hover at about one hundred meters above the van. Then they start running facial recognition. Faces start to pop up on Josh's laptop, which is sitting on the desk in the surveillance van.

Josh starts to shut the door. He sees the driver of a second small car with a long rifle. He's in line with the door that Josh has opened. One of the drones has spotted him and identifies him as being wanted for murder in Mexico. The man squeezes off a single round, and the shot strikes Josh in the neck. Jim quickly turns his attention to the man who has just shot Josh and downs him quickly with two shots, one round striking the man in his hand and the other one in his cheek. Jim turns to start returning fire on the three remaining men and is hit by a round in the left shoulder. Jim goes for cover as bullets tear into the sports car and the motor. A bullet goes through the side of the car, striking Jim in the back but not penetrating his body armor.

Brad is racing around the corner in his car. He's heading straight for the three gunmen who are continuing to fire at Jim and the van. Brad runs one of them down with his car. The other two turn and try to shoot at Brad. Jim leans out from behind the car and shoots one of the two just above the man's body armor. He dies instantly. Brad jumps out of his car, returns fire, and downs the last shooter.

• • •

Josh is trying to communicate with Brad and Jim over the headset, but his injuries are making it extremely difficult, as he's bleeding out. He sees the gunman with the long rifle start to move again, and he starts to line up a shot at Brad. Brad heads over to the van and opens the door. As he gets the door open, Josh presses the "enter" button on his keyboard, sending one of the drones off. The drone dives down and strikes the gunman in the head, killing him instantly before he can shoot at Brad.

Josh goes unconscious after saving Brad. Brad starts to administer first aid. Jim comes over. Then Mr. Daisuke and the rest of Brad's race team come out from their cover and rush over to help Brad, Jim, and Josh.

The racetrack safety team rushes over to help in administering first aid.

Seconds after the EMTs transfer Josh onto a gurney, Brad comes out of the van, holding a medium-sized go bag, and hands the bag off to Jim. His phone starts to ring inside the van.

Brad tells Jim, "Make sure Josh gets this when he wakes up." He answers with his earpiece. "PJ?"

PJ is administering first aid to Greg, "They have Rachel, Danny is critical, and Greg has some pretty bad injuries as well."

Brad struggles to keep his composure as tears start to well up. He tries to give PJ the status of all the people with him.

Brad tells him, "Josh is in critical condition. He took a round in his neck. The EMTs don't think he's going to make it. Jim took a round to the shoulder and his back. He told me that he's going to have the EMTs patch him up and he will be good to go. Now tell me what we have to do to get my wife back."

PJ says, "Their main targets were most likely Tiffany and me, not Rachel. I'll start making some calls, but I'm sure they'll contact us shortly with their demands. Then we can figure out how to get her back. She'll be fine. She's a fighter, and they're going to keep her alive if they want me."

Chapter Fourteen

Benito is waiting with Rachel on the old country road for the food truck. Benito tells his driver, Juan, "Pull over. I need you to keep an eye on the girl."

Benito gets out of the SUV and walks about fifteen feet away from the vehicle. He starts to make another phone call. Juan gets a text message and looks down at his phone quickly. Right then Rachel sees her opportunity to escape.

She grabs her belt buckle and pulls a small knife from it. Rachel starts to stab Juan in the neck multiple times. He tries to fend off her attack and tries to point his gun at Rachel, but she manages to push his arm away. He pulls the trigger, and the gunfire shatters the window on the passenger-side back door. Rachel knocks the gun out of Juan's hand. She reaches past him for the shifter and starts to put the car into gear. She starts pushing Juan's leg that's resting on the gas pedal. Benito hangs up his phone and runs back to the SUV. He opens the back door and points his gun directly at Rachel. She is still holding the knife.

Benito tells her, "You're beginning to be a real pain in my ass. I just have to keep you alive till I get PJ. That doesn't mean you can't have a few extra scars."

He aims his gun down and shoots Rachel in the leg. Rachel screams out in pain. She grabs her leg, dropping the knife by her feet. Benito reaches in and grabs the knife. Rachel takes her belt off and wraps it around the gunshot wound on her leg.

Benito receives a text; he looks down at his phone quickly and starts to smile. From down the road he sees a food truck coming toward them. Juan is bleeding severely. He stumbles out of the SUV and falls to the ground in front of Benito. The food truck comes to a stop in front of the SUV. Four men pile out, and one of them reaches down and checks the Juan's pulse.

He looks up at Benito. "He's not going to make it; he's lost too much blood."

The four men pick Juan up and put him in the back in the SUV. Then one of the men goes back to the food truck, grabs a gas jug, and starts to cover the SUV with gasoline. Benito reaches in and grabs Rachel by the back of her hair and pulls her out of the SUV. He forces Rachel into the back of the food truck. One of the four men lights the SUV on fire with his lighter.

Benito tells them, "Put the girl in the box, unless one of you wants to end up dead like Juan."

One of the men helps Rachel into a small steel box about the size of a small closet with a seat in it.

He tells Rachel, "Don't fight and you might get out of this alive."

All the men pile into the food truck and drive away.

Benito pulls out his cell phone. He pulls up the video Rachel made and sends it to Brad. One of the men start to apply first aid to Benito's injured leg.

"It looks like you got lucky. Nothing major was hit. This one's a through-and-through, and the other one is just a graze."

Benito breaks down his phone and throws the pieces out the window as they drive down the rural country road. He is handed a new phone from one of the other men in the food truck. He dials Gabriel. "Boss, you should make your way to the plane and be ready to go at a moment's notice. I sent the video. I'm going to use the boat after I get PJ for you. I'll need a vehicle waiting for me downriver. I'm sure they're going to have some kind of contingency plan."

Gabriel tells him, "I have a car being dropped off now at the boat docks for you. It should only be about a ten-minute drive to my plane from there."

"Thanks, boss; we will be seeing you soon." Benito turns to one of the men in the food truck and tells him, "Hey, you want to start making us some food? It's going to be a long night."

Rachel screams, "My husband and PJ are going to fucking kill you all. Your only chance to live is to let me go and run."

Benito motions at one of the men to shut Rachel up. As the man reaches in to slap Rachel, she grabs his arm and pulls his bracelet off his hand. Then he punches her in the face. She looks at him and smiles, with blood coming out of her nose. He shuts the door.

He turns to Benito and says, "That bitch is crazy. It's like she was happy I punched her."

Benito warns him, "Don't underestimate her. She has already killed Juan."

Inside the box Rachel opens her hands and looks down. She sees the bracelet that she has taken off the man's wrist. It's made of paracord. She begins immediately breaking down the bracelet into a small rope.

Chapter Fifteen

· · ·

Josh and Jim arrive at the hospital by helicopter. A surgical team is waiting for them at the helicopter pad. Seconds after the helicopter lands, the surgical team rushes in. They transfer Josh to a gurney and rush him into the hospital. Jim gets out of the helicopter. He is carrying the bag Brad gave him, and his AR-15 is attached to his tactical vest.

An ambulance carrying Greg and Danny pulls up in front of the hospital emergency entrance. PJ and Tyler are right behind the ambulance in PJ's Jeep. Brad rounds the corner from down the street, speeding toward the hospital. He pulls in as PJ and Tyler are getting out of the Jeep. They are setting up security around the ambulance as Greg and Danny are being helped out of the ambulance by the EMTs and the rest of the emergency staff.

Tiffany pulls into the parking lot a few seconds later in her vehicle. She is carrying a briefcase and a laptop. Rex is following behind her. Mr. Daisuke and Brad's race team pull up in the semitrailer.

Josh is being rushed to the operating room, passing a group of nurses. One of the nurses pulls out her cell phone and calls Gabriel.

Gabriel says, "Tell me you have some good news, Selena."

Selena tells him, "Good news, honey; I think I'm going to work some overtime in the ER."

Gabriel says, "Can you finish the job?"

"Honey, that sounds fun, but it's probably going to be pretty expensive."

"Check your account. That should be more than enough to cover it."

Gabriel hits "enter" on his laptop and transfers money to Selena's bank account. She gets a notification that she has received a transfer. She looks down at her phone and smiles and then puts the phone back up to her ear. "Looks like I'm going to be busy for a while."

She hangs up the phone and places it back in her pocket, then puts on some rubber gloves and walks over to start assisting with Danny's medical care.

Captain Charlie comes in the emergency entrance following everybody else, with two other police officers.

He walks right over to PJ. "Is this what you were expecting?"

"It's not over yet. They have Rachel."

Tiffany walks over to join the conversation. "I'm going to get set up and start running facial recognition. I'll let you both know if anybody pops. Captain Charlie, I'm going to need to access to their computer system."

Tiffany puts on a special pair of sunglasses with one lens that is a digital screen that reads people's faces. She walks over to the nurses' station and plugs in her laptop to one of their computers. The laptop instantly takes control of the computers. She brings up all the security cameras in the hospital and starts running facial recognition.

Selena starts to inject the IV with a syringe full of some drugs. The doctor who's working on Danny yells, "Code Blue! Get the paddles; we're starting to lose him."

Multiple doctors and nurses arrive at Danny's bedside to assist. Selena has gone to get the cart that has the defibrillator paddles on it. Her face pops up on the glasses Tiffany is wearing and also on the laptop screen. The facial recognition program puts a red box around her face and starts laying out details. She has multiple aliases and is wanted for questioning on multiple deaths in hospitals and nursing homes.

Tiffany stands up and yells at PJ, "That nurse! Get her!" She points to Selena. Tiffany runs over and tackles Selena. A few small vials and syringes fall out of her pocket as both women fall to the ground. They both stand up quickly. Selena starts to fight back, striking Tiffany in the face. Tiffany counters by punching her. The two girls wrestle to the ground, fighting each other.

PJ picks up one of the vials and hands it over to the doctor, who immediately looks at the IV and sees that Selena had started to inject Danny with a drug.

The doctor yells, "Stop that IV!"

Tiffany gets the upper hand in the fight and knocks out Selena. As Tiffany sits on top of her, Captain Charlie tosses over a pair of handcuffs. Tiffany puts the handcuffs on Selena as the two policemen come over. They pick Selena up off the ground and take her away.

Brad comes out of the elevator after checking on Josh. He looks at his phone and notices he has missed a message. He stops next to PJ, opens his phone, and plays it. PJ and Brad are focused on his phone, watching the video.

It is Rachel reading from a letter. "These are the last words you'll ever hear from me unless you have PJ come with us unarmed. They are willing to trade me for PJ at the farmers' market at 11:45 tomorrow. Or I will be put to work. They will call you tomorrow at 11:45 sharp with further instructions. Ask PJ what I mean by put to work."

Brad is in shock after the video stops playing. He's just staring at Rachel on the screen. PJ puts his hand on Brad's shoulder. "I will get her back," he says. He turns to Captain Charlie. "Tell me everything you know about the downtown farmers' market."

"I think I should probably deputize everyone before anything else happens."

"That would be a great idea."

Brad slowly walks over and sits down in a chair. He starts wiping tears away from his eyes, then looks up at PJ. A young woman comes running into the emergency room. She sees Brad sitting in the chair. She runs over and slaps Brad in the face.

She says, "You promised me that there was no way he would get hurt inside that van."

Brad turns to see that it's Josh's girlfriend, Amanda. "They have Rachel."

Amanda's demeanor changes immediately from rage to concern. She sits down next to Brad. Greg sees Brad sitting over in the waiting room. He stands up and starts to walk over to him. A nurse is trying to work on his hand and says, "Sir, you need to let me take care of your hand." She is confused as to why Greg does not seem to care about his own well-being.

Greg tells Brad, "I know things seem like everything is completely fubared right now. But just give PJ and me a little bit of time, and we'll get her back for you."

The nurse walks Greg back to the hospital bed he came from.

A doctor comes out of an elevator and walks over to the nurses' station. One of the nurses points over to Amanda, and the doctor walks over to her. "Are you Amanda?"

She fights to get her emotions under control. "Yes."

"Well, I have some good news. We got Josh stabilized, and I'm going to be moving him into a room. You can see him shortly. He did lose a lot of blood, but I do think he will make a full recovery. The bullet nicked his artery, but we were able to repair it. He was extremely lucky. Whoever helped with his first aid probably saved his life."

Amanda looks down at Brad's hands and sees blood. "Are you OK?"

Brad looks down at his hands and sees that they are still covered in blood. He reaches over and grabs a tissue and starts trying to clean them off. He remembers the moment he opened the door and saw Josh.

Brad saw Josh bleeding from his neck profusely. Josh was trying to stop the bleeding with his left hand. Brad quickly grabbed the first aid kit off the back wall of the van and started to run an IV for Josh. Brad reached down into a small refrigerator and pulled out an IV bag full of O-negative blood. He hooked up the blood to the IV line. The EMTs came rushing over to the surveillance van and took over administering first aid to Josh. Brad and the EMTs moved Josh to a gurney and started to move him over to the helicopter that was landing. Brad went back into the van and started packing up a bunch of Josh's VR equipment into a medium-sized bag. He came out the side door of the surveillance van and ran over to Jim.

Brad yelled out to Jim over the loud noise of the helicopter coming down, "Make sure Josh gets this when he wakes up." He handed the bag to Jim. "I will see you at the hospital."

Jim took the bag from Brad, turned, and started running to the helicopter. Brad looked down at his hands and saw that they were covered in blood. His phone begins to ring.

"Brad," Amanda puts her hand on his shoulder, "you should go wash your hands."

Brad gets up to go to the bathroom and starts to wash his hands. As he reaches under the sensor for the paper towels, the light doesn't come on, and there are no paper towels. Brad slaps the dispenser, knocking it off the wall. He leaves the bathroom and comes up to the nurses' station. "Who do I talk to about property damage? I broke your paper towel dispenser in the bathroom."

Jim comes out of an elevator after getting patched up by the doctors. He walks over to PJ and Charlie. "Brad's probably going to be the one telling stories at the next meeting. I'm sure glad you've been working with him. All that training you've been doing with him really paid off today."

Chapter Sixteen

— · · · —

Gabriel is sitting in his private jet. He is on the phone with Tom.

Tom says, "I just wanted to thank you again for helping me with my dad."

"Your father's helped me expand my empire over the years. That kind of loyalty gets rewarded. Make sure you two get the new distribution hub set up quickly."

"As soon as we get set up in Arizona, we will get you back on schedule."

"Now let me talk to Ross."

Tom hands the phone to Ross, Gabriel's attorney, who says, "Yeah, boss."

Gabriel tells him, "Make sure they have all the paperwork for their new identities. I trust that you have signed the documents and filed them. When you die, your family is going to be very well taken care of."

As Ross is listening to Gabriel, he starts to cough. He covers his mouth with a handkerchief. When he pulls the handkerchief away from his mouth, he looks down and sees blood in it. "Thank you, Gabriel," he says. "My family will greatly appreciate what you are doing for me."

Gabriel tells him, "I will have my guys make it as quick and painless as possible. Now put Tom back on."

"Hello," says Tom.

Gabriel tells him, "As soon as you're done identifying the body, catch up with your dad, and make sure you have no contact with anybody else. Only use cash and the new identities after you leave."

"OK, we'll be in contact shortly after we get everything set up."

The phone call ends, and Tom looks over at Ross, who is still looking down at the handkerchief.

"So how bad is it?" asks Tom.

Ross tells him, "Stage four lung cancer, and the doctors only gave me about two more months."

Tom says, "My dad and I greatly appreciate your sacrifice."

Ross nods his head and says, "I'll have your dad take my car. You can catch up with him in Arizona. It will be at least two days before they let you identify my body. Just make sure you tell them I'm your dad. That way they can close the case with your dad, and nobody will be looking for him. I've already taken care of everything. All you have to do is keep up appearances for your family and mine. Everything will be OK. A few short hours, and your dad will be on the road. Now you should go home and wait for the call. I'll tell your dad that you're looking forward to seeing him in Arizona. Saying goodbye to my family took a little longer than I thought, and I'm running late. I better get going; your dad's expecting me soon."

Tom opens the door and exits Ross's car, then walks back to his car. He starts to make a phone call, and a prison guard answers. "Hello."

Tom tells him, "Put him on."

The guard passes the phone through the jail cell bars to Chris, who says, "Is everything going as planned?"

Tom tells him, "Ross is on his way now. Take his car to the safe house. I have everything ready for you there. Your new SUV is there, full of supplies and extra fuel. I just want to get you out of state as soon as possible in case he changes his mind."

. . .

Ross is sitting in a private room. The door opens and Chris comes through the door, escorted by a prison guard.

The guard says, "You only have forty-five minutes till shift change. You'll need to make this quick."

"I was beginning to wonder if you were going to make it," says Chris.

Ross tells him, "I just wanted to tie up a few loose ends. I wanted my wife and kids to understand."

"I'm sure that was an interesting conversation."

"They understand what's best for them after I'm gone."

Ross and Chris start taking off their clothes. Chris starts putting on Ross's suit as Ross starts putting on the prison uniform. He stops getting dressed as he starts to cough. Chris hands him his shirt. Ross coughs into the T-shirt. The door opens as the prison guard comes into the room.

The prison guard says, "We need to get going."

Chris finishes putting the suit on, and Ross finishes putting the prison uniform on.

Chris tells Ross, "I guess this is where we part ways."

"I told Tom I'll have you call him after you hit the road," says Ross.

Chris starts to walk out the door, leaving Ross sitting there in the chair. A second prison guard enters and escorts Ross out of the room and down the hallway. The jail cell bars close behind them. They go down another hallway and through another set of jail cell bars. Ross is walked through, and they close behind him. He has just entered the general population area of the prison. He is greeted by several men, and they walk with him to a jail cell. One of the inmates extends his hand for Ross to shake.

The inmate says, "Your cell is that one next to us. I think we should give him at least an hour head start. Any time after that will be OK. Just let me know when you're ready. I'll make it quick."

Chapter Seventeen

— · · · —

Back at the hospital, Brad, PJ, Tiffany, Greg, Danny, and all the men from the therapy group are gathered in a hospital room, signing some paperwork for Captain Charlie. He tells them, "I'll get these filed today. At least now you guys will have more resources at your disposal. Let's not destroy this city, especially since you all work for it now."

His phone starts to ring. He looks down at it. The caller ID says, "Federal Penitentiary." He answers the phone and hears sirens going off in the background.

The warden says, "Hey, Charlie, I'm going to need to have you send SWAT out as soon as possible. We have at least one inmate dead and multiple others injured. We're having a hard time getting containment of a few areas of the prison."

Captain Charlie tells him, "A situation is developing here in town right now. But I can send you as many officers as I can spare."

Charlie hangs up the phone as he exits the hospital room.

PJ starts planning. "Tyler, I'm going to need you on overwatch."

Tyler says, "OK, then I'm going to need your Jeep."

PJ hands his keys over to Tyler and says, "Greg, I'm going to want you here at the hospital with Danny and Josh."

Greg tells him, "OK, but if you need anything else, I'm there. If you need the helicopter pilot, he's a private contractor for the hospital. I hired him for the rest of the week."

"Brad and Tiffany, I need you with me at the farmers' market," says PJ. "Tiffany, as soon as you get Rachel, take her to the hospital. We don't know what condition she will be in. I'm going to need Brad tracking me. He knows how to navigate this city better than all of us. Brad, I'm going to need you to try to figure out where they're going to be exfilling and help Tyler provide overwatch. I will go with them willingly to get them away from the general population. I don't want any innocent people getting hurt. Once Rachel is free, that's when we go on offense. I'm done getting shot at. It's time we take the fight to them."

Tyler says, "Hey, PJ, let me see that map that Charlie gave you. I'm thinking the best vantage point is going to be on the highway or one of the buildings by it. I won't be able to see you at the farmers' market, but Brad, Tiffany, and Jim will have you covered there. I'll have access to the river and the highway. That should give Tiffany enough time to get Rachel out of there and Brad time to give me a heads-up where they're exfilling you."

"The overpass by First Avenue would work best for you Tyler." Brad tells him.

• • •

Around midnight the day before the farmers' market, a food truck is sitting in a parking spot over the top of a manhole cover. Sparks fly out from under the truck as one of Benito's men is grinding off the welds holding the manhole cover down. After it's removed, the men put the cover in the food truck.

A few hours later, the farmers' market is starting to get underway. A few of the other vendors are pulling their vehicles in and starting to set up their displays. PJ is on the rooftop of a building overlooking the farmers' market, looking through a spotter scope. He turns on an earpiece, puts it in his ear, and starts to talk. "OK, everybody, start looking for anything out of place. Priority one is locating Rachel. Priority two is to identify threats, isolate them, and neutralize them. We don't want any civilians getting hurt. Tiffany, how are things looking down there?"

"I'm only going to have one drone in the air for facial recognition. The other ones I'm going to park to conserve on the batteries until we need them."

Tiffany watches patrons from the surveillance van she's sitting in as people are starting to fill the market. She is manually controlling one of the drones with her cell phone. She lands it on a small ledge overlooking the farmers' market. It is on one of the buildings, about three stories up. Another drone she moves to a building directly in front of her and lands it on the third-story ledge. Then she takes control of the third drone and directs it over to another building, landing it on a second-story ledge. The fourth drone she takes control of and switches to century mode; a search tracks her from two hundred meters above as she walks through the market.

Brad starts backing his car into a parking spot on the top floor of the parking ramp next to the farmers' market. He walks around the back side of his car and opens the trunk. He puts on his backpack and opens it up, converting it to a bulletproof vest. He attaches a holster to the front chest plate and places a nine-millimeter handgun in there. He reaches in and pulls an AR-15 out of the rifle bag, then attaches it to his gear with a rifle sling.

"I'm in position," he says. "I've cleared out the parking structure. I have Charlie's guys watching my back from the ground level, covering all the entrances to the parking ramp."

PJ tells everyone, "I'm going to head down and wait for their call. When I get down there, Tiffany, I want you to switch the drone to follow me. Let me know if anybody pops on facial recognition."

Tiffany says, "OK."

Jim's walking through the market. He notices one of the manhole covers underneath the food trucks has been moved.

Jim says, "Hey, guys, take a closer look at the food truck in the middle. It's been here all night, and now I just noticed the manhole cover underneath the truck is missing."

PJ comes out of the front door of the building whose roof he's been standing on. Jim passes PJ on the street.

PJ tells him, "I left my rifle on the roof for you. See what you can do if Brad must reposition. Charlie, can you see if those sewer lines come out anywhere but the river and try to set up some of your guys to intercept if we need to? But make sure they stay out of sight if they're leading me to the water. I'll have Brad and Tyler there to cover me."

Captain Charlie tells him, "I'll get with the city works department, but all of our manhole covers should have been welded down."

PJ says, "Brad, Tyler, move to the river—that's most likely their exfill. Tiffany, try to get a closer look at that food truck."

Tiffany, with Rex by her side now, walks over and gets in line as the market starts to open. The drone recognizes one of the people coming out the back door of the food truck. He is unloading a big metal crate to the ground with a dolly. Tiffany sits down at a nearby table and takes over the manual controls. She directs the drone around the back side of the truck while the door is open and lowers it a little bit, getting a clearer view of the inside. Her facial recognition software places red boxes over all the faces of the employees in the truck and brings up the information with all of their rap sheets.

Tiffany says, "Well, guys, we have our douchebags. There is no sign of Rachel, but that metal box that they just unloaded seems more than big enough to hold her."

PJ says, "Jim, cover Tiffany. That box contains Rachel, and most likely it contains explosives. Don't let them detonate it."

PJ's phone starts to ring. "Showtime, people. I'll be off comms from now on, but I'll still hear everything. I'm not going to do anything until Rachel is safe."

PJ answers the phone. "Hello."

It's Benito. "Go to the Cantina food truck's back door."

PJ says, "I'm not going anywhere until I have proof of life for Rachel."

Benito tells him, "You'll have your proof of life."

Inside the metal box, Rachel is using the paracord to pull on wires inside a small box she's sitting on. The wires are connected to a cell phone and a bomb. She manages to feed the paracord into the small box and then loop it around the plug and feed it back through the box; then she pulls it tight, unplugging the cell phone from the bomb. The cell phone slides to the front of the box. She can see the phone, but she cannot reach it. Her hand is just a little too big to fit through the opening. The man wheeling the box out on the dolly sets it down. The cell phone slides out of Rachel's line of view.

"No, no, damn it," she mutters. She slams her hand against the side of the metal box. In an opening in the square, the man leans in close.

He tells her, "Everybody will be seeing you soon. Maybe a little bit over there, maybe some over there, and a bit more over there."

Tiffany starts talking over her comms. "Going to need your help, Jim. The man dropping the box—when he walks away, take him out as he passes that empty bench. I'll do the rest."

Tiffany is buying a small throw blanket from one of the vendors. The man pulls out his phone as he walks away from the box. He starts texting Benito: "Everything's in place, heading to the boat now." He sends the text.

Benito receives the text, then opens the back door to the truck. PJ is standing there.

Chapter Eighteen

· · ·

Benito looks at PJ and points to the box, he says, "I'll give you two options, but they both end with you coming with me. Option one—here's the key to the box that Rachel's in. They can release Rachel after we have left. Option two—I make a phone call, and you'll see her everywhere. Now get in the fucking truck."

Benito throws the key at PJ, who catches it and sets it on the ground in front of him. Benito and one other man point their guns directly at him. Benito throws him a pair of handcuffs.

PJ says, "If you're planning on me climbing down into the sewers, I'm probably going to need my hands free."

Benito tells him, "That's where we differ. I don't care if you climb down or fall. Either way you're going down there. Now put the fucking handcuffs on."

PJ puts the handcuffs on his wrists and climbs into the back of the food truck.

•   •   •

Tiffany and Rex start walking toward the box that Rachel is in. She is coming up behind the man who dropped off Rachel. Jim takes his shot, shooting the cartel member directly through the heart. As he collapses, Tiffany grabs him, throws the blanket around him, and sits him down on the bench. She takes off the hat she was wearing and puts it over his face. Then she turns and starts heading back toward the box. Rex signals to Tiffany that there are explosives present in the box. She taps on the side of the box.

Tiffany says, "Rachel? Can you hear me?"

Rachel answers, "Yeah, I can hear you. But you need to get away from me. I'm pretty sure there's a bomb underneath me."

"Can you see it?"

"No, not very well, but I think I have already disconnected the cell phone from it."

"Nice job. Now do you see any wires connected to the door?"

"No, but there's not much light."

"OK, give me a second while we figure this out. PJ, try to keep him talking about Rachel's box. See if there are any secondary ways to set off the bomb. Tell him you're concerned about innocent people."

PJ starts to talk to Benito. "You probably rigged the door to blow once my guys open it, didn't you? That key is useless."

Benito tells him, "No, the key is good. I figured that way I could take one of your pieces off the playing field while they're tending to her."

Benito shows him the manhole cover and tells him, "I will see that you have a warrior's death for this. You know Rachel will live as long as you don't fight us."

Benito hands the phone to Amir, the other man in the food truck. Then he flips a switch next to him, arming the truck, which is wired with explosives. Amir flips a small sign around. The sign reads, "Sorry, we're closed."

Benito tells Amir, "I will text you once we're on the plane. Then you can let them have the girl. We'll see you at home. But if anybody tries to free her or kill you before you get my text, kill her and everybody in the square."

Benito leans over, opens a small panel, and flips a switch. Then he closes the panel, locking it, when he's finished. He hands the key to Amir. "I'll see you next week."

PJ says, "Do you really want to kill all these people by blowing up this food truck? All for a few extra zeros in your bank account?"

"It's not just about the money, not since you guys killed his son," says Benito. "Who do you think is going to be running everything very soon? Since you killed his son, all he has wanted is revenge. Once I can give that to him, he's going to step down and make me the next head of the cartel. I guess I should probably thank you for that."

Tiffany says, "Listen up, everybody. Secondary bomb in the food truck. Do not engage Rachel until we can neutralize the truck. Rachel has possibly neutralized the receiver for the first bomb that she's sitting on, but she cannot confirm. Let's focus on the truck."

Benito says to PJ, "Time to go."

Benito points to the manhole cover that's opened through a hole in the floor. "After you."

PJ starts to climb down the manhole into the sewer system.

Brad says, "PJ, I'm moving to the bridge on Third Avenue now. I'll cut them off; I'm going downstream. Tyler, move to the highway. It's going to be your best vantage point to provide support."

Brad gets in his GTR. He starts to race down the parking ramp. Brad begins to call Charlie on his phone.

Captain Charlie answers, "Hello."

"Charlie, they have two bombs at the market. One is in the middle of the square, with Rachel in it, and the other with the food truck. Tiffany is working on the bombs. But we're going to need you to clear the market out as soon as Tiffany neutralizes the man in the food truck."

Tiffany chimes in on the conversation. "Just give me some time to neutralize their cell phones first. Hey, Josh, do you have a cell phone jammer in the surveillance van?"

Josh struggles to talk. "I do."

Brad comes to a stop on the bridge overlooking the river. Brad gets out of his car. He takes aim, looking through his rifle scope upriver. Brad sees a boat running next to an opening for the sewer system. "Tyler," he says, "I'm in position."

"I see you. No moving at the opening yet. Wait a minute, here we go."

PJ is being escorted out of the sewer system by Benito. They get on the boat.

Benito says, "Where's Martinez?"

Fernando, one of Benito's men who was waiting on the boat, says, "I haven't seen him."

Benito says, "Looks like your team works fast."

Tiffany is running out of the surveillance van with a small box with multiple antennas on it. Rex is following her. She sets up the cell phone jammer next to the food truck back door.

Tiffany says, "The cell phones in the food truck are neutralized. We will still have our comms."

"Hook him up," says Benito. "We need to get moving." He sends off a quick text to a small group of men waiting in a car a few blocks away.

Fernando draws his gun and points it at PJ. He points to a spot at the front of the boat for PJ to sit down. On the floor of the boat in front of PJ, there are two forty-five-pound weights attached to a chain. Fernando begins to wrap the chains around PJ's waist and attaches them with a padlock. He picks up the two weights and attaches them to the side of the boat overhanging the water.

Chapter Nineteen

Tiffany walks with Rex over to a vendor selling big floppy hats. She quickly buys a hat with cash. As Tiffany starts walking over to the food truck again, she undoes a few more buttons on her top, exposing more of her breasts. She taps on the food truck window with money in her hand.

The man inside opens the window. "We're closed."

Tiffany is trying her best to hide her face with the big floppy hat, "All I need is some water for my dog."

The man stands up from the chair that he's in and starts to lean out a little bit. Tiffany's big hat is covering most of her face. He looks down at her breasts and leans over a little more. At that moment Jim takes the shot, striking the man in the head with a single round from the rifle. Tiffany and Rex turn and start running toward the box that Rachel's in.

Tiffany tells Rachel, "As soon as I open this door, do not move; we need to make sure you're not on a pressure switch."

"OK."

Tiffany draws her gun from underneath her shirt. She shoots the lock off the outside of the box. People start to run.

Captain Charlie radios out, "OK, people, we got two possible bombs, one is the Cantina food truck in the center of all the food trucks, and the secondary device in the box in the middle of the square. We need to clear the market immediately. Dispatch, I need bomb squad rolling now. I need a four-hundred-foot perimeter set. The only people allowed within the perimeter are PJ's unit and the bomb squad. Let's move, people; this is not a drill."

Jim's voice comes over the comms. "You have a small group of people heading your way; looks like one of them is heading toward the truck."

"You need to stop them," says Tiffany. "Rachel and I don't have any cover here. I'll use the drones if I have to." She opens the door on the box slowly and starts looking underneath Rachel, using her cell phone as a flashlight. "OK, it looks like it's on a timer. The cell phone is just a secondary trigger. We don't have time to diffuse it. But we can get you out of here."

"I have Rachel," she says over her comms. She starts to help Rachel out of the box. "We're heading to the hospital."

At that moment a few bullets start tearing through the box that Rachel was sitting in. Jim quickly finds the shooter through his scope and squeezes off a round, downing him instantly. The other three men open fire. One of the men directs his fire toward Tiffany and Rachel by the box. Another round tears through the box that Rachel and Tiffany are frantically trying to take cover behind.

Tiffany says, "These guys are starting to piss me off." As she pulls out her cell phone and starts to target the three remaining gunmen with the drones, Jim takes down one of the gunmen. Two of the drones take off from their ledges. The drone hovering above her strikes the gunman shooting at them and hits him in the head, killing him instantly. The remaining gunman grabs a woman running away from everything that's going on. He points his gun at the woman's head.

Tiffany says, "I can't get him with the drone without possibly hurting her."

"I got you," Jim tells her. He lines up his shot and shoots the gun out of the gunman's hand. The gunman falls back and loses his grip on his hostage. Tiffany sends the drone in, striking him in the head, and kills him instantly.

Tiffany says, "I think we're all clear. There are only a few minutes left on the timer. Charlie, I hope you got everybody clear."

Rachel, Tiffany, and Rex start running away from the box to the surveillance van.

As they get into the surveillance van, Tiffany starts talking over their comms. "We're safe, PJ."

• • •

PJ raises his hands over his head, pulling the handcuffs tight. "A little help, boys."

Tyler lines up his shot. He shoots the chain holding the handcuffs together, freeing PJ's hands. Brad lines up a shot on the chain holding the weights to PJ as the boat turns abruptly. He misses the shot. PJ starts to disarm and fight Fernando on the boat. The boat starts heading downstream at full throttle. Benito starts to shoot at PJ, but PJ uses Fernando as a shield. Fernando is hit by five out of the six shots. The sixth shot strikes PJ in the lower right side just below his ribs underneath his vest. He drops Fernando.

PJ says, "You're probably thinking to yourself, I wish I had a few more rounds."

"No," says Benito as he sets his revolver down by the steering wheel. "I was just wondering how well a one-legged man is going to swim with ninety pounds strapped to his waist."

PJ looks back at the weights attached to the side of the boat overhanging the water. Benito pulls a small lever on the dashboard of the boat, releasing the two weights into the water and pulling PJ off the boat with them. PJ grabs the side of the boat as he starts to go overboard. He hangs onto the edge, trying to pull himself back up. As PJ looks up, he sees Brad on the bridge. Benito quickly reloads his revolver and aims it at PJ, who lets go of the boat as it goes under the bridge.

Brad sees PJ let go. He yells, "Greg, I need the helicopter here now, Third Avenue bridge. PJ just went in the water with some weights tied to him. I'm going in. Josh, don't let him get away."

Brad's car takes off across the bridge and around the corner, following the boat in the river. Brad dives off the bridge, swims down, and finds PJ carrying the weights across the bottom of the riverbed toward the bank. He grabs the chain holding PJ to the weights, then pulls his handgun from the ballistic vest that he's wearing and shoots the chain twice. PJ and Brad swim up for air. As they come to the surface of the water, they start swimming to the riverbank. Brad starts to catch his breath at the riverbank.

"We're not done yet," says PJ. "Our ride just showed up." He points at the helicopter coming down. The bombs go off, echoing through the farmers' market and the downtown buildings. The explosion sets off multiple alarms and shatters windows in many of the buildings. There is a lot of damage done to multiple cars, rocking the surveillance van as Tiffany is driving it away from the area with Rachel and Rex in it. The helicopter pilot starts coming down above the river. He begins to hover above the riverbank as Brad and PJ climb into the helicopter. Greg hands PJ a rifle.

Brad says, "Josh, tell me you haven't lost him."

Josh is driving Brad's car with the use of a virtual reality headset and a radio control attached to a laptop.

Josh is still struggling to talk. "He's heading south, downriver. But it looks like he is heading into the boat ramp. It looks like he has a car waiting for him."

Josh stops Brad's car by the side of the road leading to the boat ramp. Benito turns the boat into the ramp and docks it. A man at the dock goes to tie up the boat and hands Benito keys to a car. Benito gets into a brand-new Corvette and speeds out of the parking lot and down the road. The helicopter catches up to Brad's car. Brad points down to his car. The helicopter pilot starts to land a few feet away from it. Brad jumps out of the helicopter and gets into his car, then quickly takes control of it by switching off the remote option.

Brad tells Josh, "I'll take it from here."

The helicopter takes off as Brad starts accelerating down the road to catch Benito.

"Where in the hell is he going?" asks Brad over the comms. "They have to know I'm going to catch them."

The helicopter pilot says, "Last month I was flying over the old Whitmore farm, and whoever bought the place was putting in a new driveway. It would definitely be big enough for a plane to land."

"PJ, think you guys can find a good spot to provide overwatch for me?" asks Brad. "I got an idea on how to draw out whoever's been pulling his strings."

The helicopter pilot starts pushing the helicopter to its limits, speeding ahead. Brad catches up with Benito's car quickly. Benito notices Brad catching up to him in the rearview mirror. He pulls the revolver from his waistband and sets it on the seat next to him. Then he reaches to open the glove box, revealing another gun. He grabs the gun, turns, and starts shooting at Brad in his car. Brad moves his GTR to the rear passenger side of Benito's car and starts to perform a pit maneuver, forcing the Corvette to lose control. Benito's car crashes into the ditch in front of the old Whitmore farm. Brad

makes the turn into the driveway and starts making do-
nuts on the extremely long and wide driveway. Benito
starts to climb out of his overturned vehicle. He is badly
hurt. He shoots at Brad's car.

Gabriel yells, "Go kill that son of a bitch and get
him off my runway. I need to leave."

Two men get off the airplane and open the barn
doors. The pilot starts the jet engines. The plane starts to
taxi out of the barn. PJ is on a small hill overlooking the
farm, with the sun at his back and the helicopter parked
beside him. PJ squeezes off a round, killing Benito. PJ
takes aim at one of the two men Gabriel told to kill
Brad. One of them opens fire, striking Brad's wheel and
blowing out the tire. He continues shooting at Brad's
car. The second round manages to tear through the
driver's side rear tire. The tire quickly comes apart off
the rim, disabling Brad's GTR. More bullets continue
to tear into the car, striking the windshield and driver's
side window. The bullets are stopped by the bullet-resis-
tant material put on the car and windows earlier. Brad
scrambles to get to the passenger side and out of the car.
He takes cover behind the passenger side door after he
shuts it. PJ shoots and takes out the man shooting at
Brad's car. The second man sees PJ on the top of the hill
overlooking the farm.

The gunman turns to Gabriel and tells him, "You need to leave now boss. Your plane should be able to get by the car. I'm going to need my rifle."

Gabriel reaches over and grabs the rifle and a few magazines out of a black box full of rifles. He hands them over as he is shutting the door.

Gabriel turns to the pilot and yells at him, "What are you waiting for? Let's go."

The pilot starts taxing the plane out the barn slowly. The gunman starts climbing up higher into the barn. The gunman opens a small door leading to the roof and climbs through it. Brad grabs the drone out of his car, turns it on, and starts flying it toward the plane. "Josh," he asks. "Does this thing have a payload on it?"

Josh says, "No, it has an extra lithium-ion battery. That one is only meant for surveillance."

Brad says, "PJ, start punching a few holes in that left wing. Once I get the drone close enough, you can shoot the battery on the drone. Hopefully that will be enough to short the battery and ignite the jet fuel coming out of the wing."

PJ says, "It's worth a shot. At the very least, we're going to cut his range down on that plane. He probably won't be able to make it back to Mexico."

PJ starts rapidly shooting at the left wing, punching several holes through it, and fuel starts to pour out of the holes. The plane starts to take off as the drone catches up to it. PJ lines up the shot on the drone. He waits until the drone starts to come in contact with the fuel coming off the wing. He shoots the battery on the drone, causing it to explode. It ignites the fuel coming out of the wing. The wing catches fire and explodes. The plane starts to lose elevation quickly and crashes into the large field. The man on the rooftop of the barn struggles to line up his shot with the sun in his face. Greg sees the reflection off the sniper scope on the roof of the barn.

"Shooter on top of the barn," says Greg.

The gunman's round strikes the ground in front of PJ. Brad turns quickly from hearing the gunshot. Brad sees the gunman on the roof and grabs his AR-15 from inside his car. The gunman's second shot narrowly misses PJ's arm. Brad turns his attention to the shooter on the barn. PJ is not looking very good. He starts to lose consciousness. Brad shoots two rounds at the gunman on the roof, striking him twice. The man falls off the roof onto the ground and is killed.

Greg says, "Our government spends millions of dollars on missiles to take out planes, and you guys can do it with a rifle and a $500 drone. Now let's go clear the wreckage and make sure this is over with."

PJ doesn't respond or move. Greg taps PJ on the shoulder and sees that he's unconscious. He immediately picks him up and carries him to the helicopter. He sees that PJ has been bleeding from underneath his vest for a while now.

Greg tells the helicopter pilot, "We need to get back to the hospital now. PJ's been hit."

"I'll have Charlie send me some help to clear the crash site," says Brad. "I'll see you guys in the hospital shortly." He turns on his cell phone and speed-dials Charlie. "Charlie, I'm going to need some help to clear the crash site at the old Whitmore farm. PJ is en route back to the hospital. He's been shot. How's Rachel doing?"

"OK. I'm going to send a couple units. The doctor said she is doing good, and he expects her to make a full recovery. Now what the hell do you mean, crash site?"

Chapter Twenty

— • • • —

On the helipad back at the hospital, the emergency response team is starting to load PJ onto a gurney.

The doctor says, "I need a full medical history. I need two lines of O-negative going now."

As the hospital staff starts to turn PJ, they notice a scar on his lower back.

The nurse says, "He has a scar consistent with a kidney surgery and a gunshot exit wound on his right flank."

"We need to confirm that he has lost a kidney before I have to take this one," says the doctor. The medical staff start to wheel him into the hospital.

• • •

Brad comes into the emergency entrance of the hospital, still in his tactical gear, with his firearms strapped to him. Tiffany, Rex, and Greg greet him. Tiffany walks with Brad to the elevator and tells him, "Rachel is in room 319. You should be proud of her. She never stopped fighting. PJ is still in surgery."

Brad starts jogging down the hallway to the elevators and anxiously presses the button several times to call the elevator. The doors open, and he gets in.

Over in Josh's hospital room, a nurse is talking to Josh. She is checking his IV and vital signs. "Just press the call button if you need anything."

Amanda looks over at Josh. "I'm going to go check on Rachel."

In the hallway the elevator doors open, and Brad starts running down the hallway, looking at room numbers. He almost runs into Amanda and the nurse coming out of Josh's room. "Where's Rachel's room?" he says.

Amanda tells him, "Two more rooms down, on your left."

"Thanks."

He runs to the open door of Rachel's room as Rachel is coming out of the bathroom. Brad picks her up, spinning her around and kissing her. "I will never let anyone take you away from me again."

"Put me down," she says. "Put me down."

Rachel is struggling to hold back from throwing up as she rushes back into the bathroom. A nurse walks into the room, holding a tray with medicine, crushed ice, and a cup of Jell-O for Rachel. "You must be Brad."

"Yeah. How's she doing?"

"She's doing good. She is starting to have a hard time keeping solid food down right now. But that is to be expected with a first-time pregnancy."

Brad starts to smile as he is looking at the nurse. Rachel comes out of the bathroom. She looks over at Brad.

Rachel asks him, "Why do you look so happy? I was kidnapped, shot, and almost blown up."

"I know…but you're also carrying my child." Brad grabs Rachel by the waist. He gets down on one knee and kisses Rachel on her stomach.

• • •

Captain Charlie is sitting at his desk with a huge stack of papers to his left as he's filling out paperwork. An officer knocks on the door, and Captain Charlie waves him in. The officer adds another stack of papers on top of the desk. "Captain, Tiffany is here with a couple of guys. They need to speak to you before the press conference."

Captain Charlie gets up and walks out of his office. He meets Tiffany and the two gentlemen. They walk down the hallway, and Captain Charlie opens a door to a small conference room and shuts the door behind them. One of the men hands him a small stack of note cards. Captain Charlie looks through the cards. Tiffany comes out of the conference room and starts walking back down the hallway to Captain Charlie's office. She picks up the stack of papers on his desk and brings them back to the conference room. She hands it to one of the two men leaving the room. Tiffany and Charlie stand there in the conference room.

"We can finally put an end to all of this," says Tiffany. "Now we have a press conference to get to."

Captain Charlie opens the door of the conference room for her. They both start walking down the hallway to a small press conference set up in the lobby of the police station.

Chapter Twenty-One

PJ is asleep in his hospital bed following surgery. Greg, Tyler, and Danny are all in the room with him. They are watching the live news conference on the television.

The nurse with PJ tells them, "He should be waking up soon. Let me know if he needs anything."

Captain Charlie starts to speak at the news conference. "I would like to thank everybody for being patient. We have quite a lot of information to get through. So why don't we get started? Our new antiterrorism unit has been busy, and we are extremely lucky to have them. They neutralized all the terrorists, with no loss of civilians or our personnel. They could not prevent the bombs from going off, however. They did limit the damage to a few buildings and vehicles in the blast radius."

Greg shuts off the TV. "You guys ever wonder what people would say if they knew what PJ's unit has actually been doing the past twenty years?"

Brad is in a wheelchair, wheeling himself into PJ's room.

Tyler looks up and says, "Hey." He gets up and shakes Brad's hand.

Greg asks Brad, "How's it going?" He reaches over with his good hand and shakes Brad's hand.

"I'm doing OK. How's your hand?"

"I'll be fine."

Brad looks over at Danny in his wheelchair. "Danny, how are you doing?"

"I'll manage. I'm just sorry we couldn't stop them from taking Rachel."

Brad replies to Danny, "I shouldn't have put you guys in that situation. There were just too many variables."

PJ starts to wake up, and Brad says, "Look here, boys, Sleeping Beauty finally decided to join the party."

PJ starts to talk. "I've only woken up in a hospital bed twice. Once I lost my kidney; once I lost my leg." He slowly lifts the bed sheet, looks down, and sees his bandages. "Dammit, I thought my vest took that round." As he starts to put the sheet back down, the doctor enters the room with a nurse.

"Good, you're awake. Try not to move too much, PJ. You've been through quite a lot in the last few hours, and I don't want you to tear anything loose. You got really lucky with that kidney donation."

"I think that's my cue to go, boys," says Brad.

Greg and Danny both start to chuckle and smile as Brad wheels himself out of the room and the doctor continues to explain what happened.

• • •

Captain Charlie has just finished answering questions and is walking away from the podium toward Tiffany. "Do you think we can finally put this behind us now?"

"With these kinds of people, nothing is ever done. But next time they'll definitely think twice before they come at us."

Charlie's cell phone starts to ring. It's one of the officers he sent to help with the crash site. The officer tells him, "We're just wrapping things up here. We have five dead on site. We also have recovered multiple cell phones and multiple firearms."

"Try to get all that evidence back here for the techs to go through it."

"We should be back there around five."

The officer starts putting the cell phones in a box as one of them starts to ring. The screen lights up with the message of three missed calls. On the other end of the phone, there is a young woman.

The young woman hangs up the phone and puts it down on a desk. Next to it is a pregnancy test. It shows a positive result. She looks down, and she puts her hand on her stomach.

"One day all of this will be yours. But until that day, I'll run things for you. Then we can figure out what you would like to do to the people that killed your father and your big brother."

She gets up from the big desk she is sitting behind and walks out on a big patio overlooking a massive backyard with a huge pool. Multiple security guards are walking on the grounds.

• • •

Six months later, Rachel is noticeably pregnant and sitting on a chair. She is on the phone taking a pizza order. Brad is cutting up some pizzas on a big table behind her. PJ comes in the front door of Phil's Pizza, carrying a delivery bag, as the doorbell goes off. Brad looks up and sees him.

"Are you going to hire another driver? I do have my own business to tend to," says PJ.

Brad smiles as he gazes down at the garbage can filled with a stack of applications. Rachel shakes her head at Brad. He shrugs his shoulders. "What?"

The End

Milton Keynes UK
Ingram Content Group UK Ltd.
UKHW050501280324
440101UK00017B/1318